D1562594

Murder?
A Memoir

A Cate May Mystery

Susan Sumner

Murder? A Memoir

DEDICATION

To My Three Grandchildren.

Murder? A Memoir

CONTENTS

Murder? A Memoir

Part One

Early July 2021

Murder? A Memoir

CHAPTER 1

Monday began like an ordinary day. Yoga class starts at 9:30 and I needed to hurry because I had wasted too much time reading emails. I ate a quick breakfast – a peanut butter sandwich on organic whole-grain toast, a green smoothie (kale from my garden, sorrel from Kika's garden, assorted fruit and a few herbs and spices) blended for 30 seconds in my high speed blender. After two minutes using my **Bright Smile** electric toothbrush I was ready for the day.

I was excited about yoga because it was one of the first classes to resume since the pandemic changed our world. Life had just started to get back to normal following a year of social distancing.

I put on my shoes and headed out the door. It was a hot day, a little mist in the air but not quite rain. I set out for yoga, which is in the auditorium, just a short stroll away, but today I strode quickly because, as you know, I was a little late.

In exercise class I usually sit near the entrance, in the back row on the left side of the room. I looked around the class. There were about 10 people there – all women today. My buddy Phyllis was toward the front.

Samantha was in the first row. Her bright red yoga pants and red spiky wig added a note of color to the room. She has several vibrant wigs which she coordinates with her clothes and earrings. She tells people that she chooses colors according to her daily horoscope.

A few minutes after class started Sally arrived, cheerfully asking if we like the snow. I stifled back a snort of laughter. Sally is a friendly, talkative woman who is always at least 15 minutes late. She has the beginnings of dementia and can't remember much so maybe it isn't funny - but snow in July?

We started with a few modified downward

dogs, using a chair for support. Then we did some rather shaky tree and warrior poses. I was pleased to see several people were even more wobbly than I was. Class ended with ten minutes of meditation. Some people complain that meditation is too long and their mind wanders, but it is my favorite part of class because I mentally complete my shopping list and plan for the day.

You may have noticed this isn't a typical yoga class. Maybe I should introduce myself. My name is Cate May; I live in Golden Oaks Retirement Center and all our exercise classes are "modified." But chair yoga is kind of fun and supposed to be good for balance and keeping alert mentally. I pride myself on both skills.

After yoga Phyllis and I headed back to our apartments together. Phyllis is a short energetic woman with curly white hair and a wicked sense of humor. She loves to dance and when a man moves into Golden Oaks she checks to see if he is a dancer. She jokingly says she is looking for a rich man to pay her rent.

She is 95 but acts like she's seven. She was the one who "borrowed" the big round trays from dining services to use as sleds last winter.

That sounded like a good idea to us but management was not so excited. Luckily there were no serious injuries.

Phyllis and I talked about changes at Golden Oaks. Some people had moved away to be near family, a few became more forgetful and seemed to fade away and several people had died. Phyllis said, "You know, Cate, the only problem with Golden Oaks is that friends you make here may not be around forever."

After a certain age that is probably true no matter where you live. Last fall my former neighbor Donna stopped for an unannounced visit. She didn't see the parking lot and drove up a narrow walking trail and left her car next to the gazebo. Shortly after that she told me that her daughter took away her keys, license and car. Donna was upset for weeks and threatened to have her daughter arrested. Now she seems to have forgotten she ever drove.

Another friend was on the waiting list for an apartment at Golden Oaks but never moved here. She still lives in a big house but has a full time nurse and seldom goes out. So unless you want to be a trend-setter and leave first you probably have to expect this kind of thing.

CHAPTER 2

Golden Oaks is a small retirement community in rural Rockland County, New York, about 40 miles from the city. It is built on a gentle hill that backs up to a forest with trails for walking.

I have a one-bedroom apartment in the Bluebird section. My sun-filled den opens to a view of a small golf course. Phyllis has a two-bedroom apartment in the next building. Her apartment faces the pathways so she usually knows what our neighbors are doing.

The first floor of the main building has meeting rooms, a library, a chapel and the auditorium. The second floor is called The Cloisters; it has hotel style apartments and the residents eat in the main dining room.

There are three dining rooms and the pub. Happy Hour Social with reduced-price drinks is a lively time of day. I usually skip the Socials because I don't drink. I used to drink but stopped when I realized that I was spending more time planning cocktails than meals. I tell people I'll start going to Happy Hour Social when I start to feel either happy or social.

The nursing and memory care units are on the third floor. Because I've lived here for seven years, I know people in every section of campus. It's nice to be able to stay in touch with friends who have "graduated" to another level of care.

CHAPTER 3

News about the pandemic was encouraging and the number of new cases in New York State was very low. Almost all of the residents at Golden Oaks had been vaccinated.

Phyllis, Anita and I were eager to go to a restaurant for our first trip off campus in over a year. On a sunny July day we had lunch on the patio of an upscale restaurant outside of town.

Anita was still very cautious so we kept our masks on except when we were eating, and even then Anita looked a little nervous.

Anita is 81 years old and has white hair. She is about 5'9", almost as tall as I am. In fact some people have trouble telling us apart. We really look quite different, but residents sometimes can't remember names and young people who even notice us think everyone over sixty looks alike.

Over a glass of red wine, Anita talked at length about her garden and a rare iris that she planted last fall. She pulled out her phone to show us a photo of a Hester Prynne Iris, dark purple and lavender with yellow accents. It is lovely and apparently it is endangered, very rare and possibly valuable.

Anita is a member of a group called Historic Iris (historiciris.org) which tries to save valuable or endangered iris plants by growing them in anonymous flower beds all over the country. She was happy to be able to help out and hoped to get a rhizome for Daphne Iris, another endangered iris, to plant next year.

She was planning to go to an Iris Garden on Monday; "So, want to join me? Cate? Phyllis? It'll be interesting and we can have lunch in the café there. The food there is wonderful and they use edible flowers in their salads."

I gracefully declined. My eyes had already glazed over a bit because all this talk about rhizomes went way over my head. I didn't even know what a rhizome was or how to pronounce it until today.

Phyllis managed to look mildly interested as Anita described her irises but also decided against a day at an iris garden. She grows tomatoes in the community garden and marigolds around her apartment but does not share Anita's intense interest in plants.

Then Anita mentioned that she has begun to grow herbs and she thinks they have given her more energy. My ears perked up because, as you know, I put herbs into my smoothies.

Anita said, "Do you remember my friend Joan – the one who died last August? She was a master gardener and had a plot near mine. She was the one who got me interested in herbs."

I vaguely remembered that last year Anita and Phyllis had been upset about Joan's death, but now I was more interested in hearing about the herbs than about Joan.

"What kind of herbs do you grow?" I asked. As you may have guessed, I am very health conscious and figure that any advantage is worth considering.

Anita mentioned several varieties – some familiar and others with strange names. She explained that she likes to make teas and is trying to find recipes online for combinations that would lessen her headaches.

I hinted, "I would love to have some herbs for my green smoothies – do you think they would taste good?"

"No, Cate, a lot of them need to be distilled into elixirs, not just mixed in a blender – it's a complicated process. But I can show you sometime," she added kindly.

But then she cautioned, "You have to be careful with herbs because some of them have dangerous side effects and some can actually kill you, especially if you combine them."

"Ooh," I said, "That sounds kind of interesting – keep me posted please!"

Golden Oaks has a community garden. Residents can have 10x10 foot plots or raised beds. There is periodic discussion whether to call them plots or beds – does the word "plot" sound too funereal to you?

My raised box (about 2 feet by 8 feet) eliminates the need for kneeling. I mostly grow kale, chard and bush beans and get the seeds for free from the library in town. But I could definitely make room for a few herbs and would be happy to buy seeds if this might increase my energy.

Anyway, it was good to see Anita so happy and excited because she had been having severe headaches for several months. She had recently switched to a new doctor and had undergone a series of medical tests (stress test, MRI, CAT scan and who knows what else). All the results had been good and she was feeling very relieved.

In addition to the herbal teas she was drinking, Anita was taking a new medication which seemed to be working – it's one of the ones you see advertised on TV with long lists of side effects including death, but so far so good.

CHAPTER 4

A few days later I was all set to go to Zumba class at 9:30 when the phone rang. It was Phyllis. Anita had been taken to the hospital during the night. I was surprised because she seemed so energetic and happy when we saw her at lunch. We weren't too worried because the results of her tests were so good.

I continued on to Zumba. Today Jamie was sitting in my chair. Not wanting to make a scene, I pulled another chair to the back of the room. The usual crew was there, but I noticed Samantha was absent and figured it was taking her too long to study her horoscope and determine her outfit for the day. Most of

Zumba is done sitting in a chair and seems a little silly, but it's one way I keep up my physical and mental strength – or so I tell myself.

Soon after I got home Phyllis called again crying so hard I could hardly understand her. "Cate," she sobbed, "Anita died last night." She went on to say that when the ambulance arrived at the hospital Anita's doctor happened to be there and could not believe that she had died because her test results had been so good.

People at Golden Oaks talked about nothing but Anita's death for days. Dee Dee cried every time the subject came up; her husband Joe seemed to think something very strange is going on here because several people had died suddenly at night in the past year.

Carol said, "Anita died because she always wore her mask all day long. This whole pandemic thing is exaggerated. There is no need for masks."

Dee Dee asked through sobs, "How can you say that? Do you think we will all die if we wear masks?"

Carol has very definite opinions and gives them often and loudly; some don't seem to have much medical basis as far as I can tell. She repeated more forcefully, "I was a nurse for years so I know the truth – masks can be dangerous."

Carol's long grey hair is worn in a bun. She is short and slender with a thin face that has a perpetual pout. I think she means well because she says we can call her any time if we need help.

I left after a few minutes because my grandchildren were coming about 3:00 and I had house cleaning to do before they arrived. My son and his wife were going on vacation and I was going to take care of the kids. I was excited because they are so much fun and will surely take my mind off Anita's death.

CHAPTER 5

My grandchildren Jane, Jeff and Roger (in alphabetical order) arrived as scheduled around 3:00. Their parents Gary and Elizabeth left for the Newark airport to catch a 6:00 plane to Jamaica for a second honeymoon.

Jane is 11 years old, has long dark hair and is tall, very pretty and graceful. I like to think she looks a lot like me. Roger and Jeff are 8-year-old identical twins but I can always tell them apart. All three are funny and very smart. I think those traits probably come from me.

They are very athletic. Jane pitches for her softball team and is the high scorer on her basketball team. She is also a competitive year-round swimmer. Jeff and Roger love basketball and their team never lost a game. They are also on an undefeated soccer team – Jeff is goalie and Roger plays defense.

My one-bedroom apartment seemed a little crowded with a queen size blow-up air mattress and an extra cot. But we didn't care – it would be a giant sleepover.

That afternoon we played golf on the little course in back of my house. The kids have been taking lessons; Jeff takes golf seriously and really enjoys it.

I was happy to connect with the ball on my first swing. It bounced a few feet and rolled into a clump of grass. "Don't slow the club down after you hit the ball. You need to swing all the way through to make the ball go far," Jeff advised.

They had me do several practice swings which seemed to make the ball go farther but not always in the right direction. Then Roger suggested, "Keep your eye on the ball but be sure to look at the green before you swing."

When we got to the green, my first putt sailed across it into the sand trap. Jane pointed out that a full swing was not a good idea for putting. Jeff added, "But you still need to keep your eye on the goal."

There is a driving range and mini golf course

in town and we thought it would be fun to go there tomorrow. It will be good practice and maybe my neighbors and I can play on a regular basis on our golf course. I made a mental note to mention this to Phyllis – she played 18 holes of golf every week until last year when she broke her hand.

All three kids like to cook so we decided that they would each make a meal while they were there. That night Roger made his signature pizza and it was delicious!

After supper we watched Peppa Pig which I have loved since they were very little. Today they let me watch it for old times' sake even though they have really outgrown it. Then the news came on and there was a story about a well-known scientist who died suddenly.

That made me think about Anita, so I told them about her and that she had died suddenly a few days ago. Jane is very empathetic and was sorry that I lost a friend – she seemed to take Anita's death very seriously.

Jeff (or was it Roger?) said, "Do you think that someone killed her?" Roger (or was it Jeff?) agreed there might be something going on and perhaps we should investigate. The boys had gone to a CSI (crime scene investigation) camp a few weeks ago and I thought that might have made them unnecessarily suspicious.

I asked, "What makes you think that? Why would anyone want to kill her?"

Jane said, "There can be all sorts of reasons to kill someone. You should ask to see the results of the autopsy. At least then we would know the cause of death." I don't think young children should know about autopsies, so I made a mental note to tell Elizabeth and Gary to keep a close eye on TV shows the children watch, books they read and camps they attend.

When I said that I didn't think an autopsy had been done, Jeff urged me to make sure. "You know autopsies can provide important clues."

I was a little dubious but said, "Okay, tomorrow I will talk to Mr. Andrews, he's a member of the board of directors and might know if an autopsy was done."

I am on the council at Golden Oaks – the council consists of ten residents who meet once a month with members of the board and other bigwigs. Some of them are a little intimidating, but Mr. Andrews seems quite approachable.

I called Mr. Andrews' secretary to make an appointment. She asked why I wanted to see him and accepted my explanation that I had some concerns about the previous council meeting.

After a few moments of chitchat, I got to the point and told Mr. Andrews about Anita and how upset and surprised I was that she had died so suddenly. He was certainly aware of the situation and expressed sympathy. I thought he seemed a little bit uncomfortable talking about it.

"What did the autopsy show?" I asked.

He said, "Well as you know, my dear, it's not unusual for older people to die suddenly, so there was no need for an autopsy."

I repeated that her sudden death seemed very strange to me because she was so healthy and full of life the day before. He insisted that there was nothing suspicious and therefore no reason for an autopsy. I thanked him for his time and urged him to think about this a little more.

That evening after a delicious meal of Jeff's famous mac and cheese we started talking about Anita again. I told them about my conversation with Mr. Andrews, and they did not think his answers were satisfactory. They thought there should have been an autopsy. I was beginning to think they might be right in thinking that something suspicious could be going on. We agreed this should be investigated further, and I was pleased to see they seem to have inherited my logical thinking skills.

CHAPTER 6

On Thursday morning after breakfast I told the kids they were on their own for an hour because I had to go to aerobics class. They wanted to know what exercises we did. When I said some of it was done in the chair, they could not stop laughing. I could still hear them laughing as I walked down the path.

I looked around the class at my fellow students. Most of them were in their 70s and '80s and a few were in their nineties. Could Mr. Andrews be right that people that age often die suddenly? Or could something sinister be happening?

Samantha was back in class today sporting a

bright blue wig with coordinating makeup and sparkly blue earrings. I wondered briefly what her horoscope could possibly have said that would warrant this combination. Perhaps I could talk her into presenting a program on how we can use horoscopes in our daily lives.

Carol was dressed in orange sweatpants and a very warm sweatshirt even though it was almost 80 degrees. You would think a former nurse would dress for the weather. My train of thought was interrupted when Sally arrived late and started talking about snow.

Two people in class today have walkers. Others have limited mobility because of hip, knee or shoulder problems. We do what we can in the exercise classes, and no one worries if someone isn't perfect. Most teachers are encouraging but have realistic expectations and don't push us too hard.

Our teacher today seems determined to improve our form. It's a losing battle. "Hold your arms straight up and wrap them around each other. Now stand on one foot." She waits and repeats her instructions in an annoyed voice when almost none of us can follow her example.

This particular exercise is hard for me. Two

years ago I went to a friend's house to help with her computer, which was upstairs. Coming down the stairs I missed the last step and fell and broke my right shoulder. My shoulder is much better now but not perfect.

When I tell the instructor about my shoulder she says, "If it hurts don't do it." But a few minutes later she seems to forget her own advice and pushes again for perfection.

Some people think she is a wonderful teacher, but I have noticed that they are hard of hearing and pay no attention to her instructions. I am working on changing my expectations because I can see that her exercise class is helpful.

CHAPTER 7

This afternoon my bocce team, the Nerds, was scheduled to play the Sonics. I was happy that the kids could watch me play bocce and see where they get their athletic ability.

When we got to the court I noticed Carol was sitting on the sidelines still dressed in the very warm orange sweatpants she had worn to class.

A bocce team has four players. Fred and I were at one end of the court with two members of the opposing team, Ted and Agnes. Ted is the captain of the Sonics. He is a tall, heavy set man with squinty eyes and a pinched-in face. He's very hard-of-hearing and speaks forcefully all the time. His wife, Agnes, is pleasant but seems to blend into the background.

Alex and Ginny were at the other end of the court. Alex is the captain of my team; he had just returned from a trip to Florida to see his daughter and grandchildren, and his tan looked very dark against his white hair. He walks with a slight limp but this does not affect his bocce skill.

When his end of the court wasn't playing, Alex sat on the bench next to the kids and I saw them laughing together. I was glad they seemed to be having fun.

My team started off strong. Alex is the high scorer at most games and he and Fred were both playing very well. Ginny is always a steady player.

Throughout the game Ted complained very loudly to his wife about our team: "Alex is their only decent player. They wouldn't stand a chance without him." After one of Alex's shots bounced off the side and roared past the pallino, Ted grumbled, "He's very overrated. I don't know why he is the head of the whole league." Another time he muttered that something had changed the odds and seemed almost gleeful as he spoke.

He also bad-mouthed his own team, "We'd be better off without Tom. His shots are way off this year. And Joanne isn't much better. We wouldn't win any games at all if it wasn't for me."

He made me so nervous that one of my shots rolled exuberantly past the pallino and knocked Fred's ball out of position before crashing at the end of the court. Ted turned to his wife and demanded loudly, "Did you see that? People should have some skills if they're going to play on these teams."

His wife looked at me apologetically but said nothing. I guess silence is the better part of valor if you live with Ted.

In the end the Sonics beat us by five points. I hate to admit that I was pretty upset by the loss.

When I got back home Jane said, "Sit down and relax, Grandma." She prepared a delicious pasta dinner for us, and I felt much better after eating. This was her specialty and one of my favorite meals ever.

The children told me not to worry about the game. Roger said, "You weren't terrible. I think you're better at bocce than you are at golf."

"Your last shot almost came close to that little yellow ball," Jeff said kindly. He added "Maybe you'll get better the more you play." This is probably good advice. I have noticed that when Jeff decides to do something he keeps at it and usually succeeds. He almost mastered Rubik's cube last year.

Sometimes they call me Grandma Daddy – Jane started calling me this when she was two years old because I'm their dad's mom. Roger shortened it to Grand, probably because I'm such a grand person.

Roger asked, "Grand, why was that lady taking notes at your game?" I was a little puzzled at first. When he described the orange sweatpants, I said, "Oh that's Carol. I see her in execise class but I have no idea why she was at the bocce game." I went on, "She used to be a nurse – maybe she thinks someone might need medical help." Although I was joking, there might be some truth to this – she seems very impressed with her nursing skills.

We agreed that it was a little weird for anyone to take a bocce game so seriously that they keep notes. "Come to think of it, she was doing that last week too." I replied. For some reason a chill ran down my spine.

CHAPTER 8

The next few days passed pleasantly, playing golf and swimming. We have a heated salt-water pool, and I enjoy meeting friends there in the afternoon. I told the kids they would need to be careful if other residents were in the pool. No cannonballing or diving at Golden Oaks.

I may not have mentioned that the kids are all on swim teams and have lots of trophies and ribbons. Today they enjoyed racing each other in the right lane of the pool. I decided that was ok because Phyllis and I were the only ones in the water and we were chatting in the left-hand corner of the pool. A few residents were sitting around the pool reading or gossiping.

"Oh, no!" I said, "Look who just arrived!"

Phyllis took a quick look and said, "Oh my goodness, there goes our day!"

It was Ted, who had been so obnoxious at the bocce game the other day. He has lived here at least eight years and has managed to alienate almost everybody. He berates the staff if anything displeases him. During Sunday brunch, he elbows people to get ahead of them in the line. He dominates the discussion of every group he joins. Most of us try to avoid him.

Today Ted looked around the pool and said, "What are those children doing here?"

"They're swimming." I replied in what I hoped was a condescending tone.

"Do you know them? If so, please ask them to leave. This pool is for residents only. You should be aware of that, Cate," he snarled.

I said, "Ted, they are my guests and have every right to be here."

There were several empty lanes in the pool, but he got in the left lane and barreled right toward Phyllis and me.

The three kids stopped swimming and came

over to us. Jane asked, "What is he doing? That man is dangerous!"

We got out of the water, giving Ted the whole pool to himself; he only swam two laps then got out to sit in the sun and fell asleep almost immediately.

Skoota Man rolled in while Ted was sunning himself. His real name is Jack but everyone calls him Skoota Man because he zips around in a motorized scooter.

I waved to Skoota Man and he came over to join us. I introduced him to the kids and the boys were very impressed by his scooter. He made a joke about Ted and I told him what had happened.

"Would you like me to run him over?" Skoota Man asked.

We all laughed, but I thought it was a good idea and said, "That would make a lot of people very happy."

Skoota Man and his wife are both excellent bocce players; their team has won the championship for several years. They give bocce lessons on Saturdays and I keep meaning to go to a lesson but somehow never get around to it.

"Yes, Ted is obnoxious but he does have

some good points." Skoota Man said. I raised a skeptical eyebrow.

"Ted works in the woodshop with me. He makes wooden toys for the children in Little Acorn and he makes the birdhouses you see around campus. He really works very hard and takes it seriously."

I probably looked doubtful because Skoota Man continued, "Anyway, we'll get a break from him for a while because he's going to visit his son in Maine sometime soon." This was welcome news indeed.

It always amazes me how some people complain about everything and others seem to handle significant problems with grace and strength.

.

CHAPTER 9

Just before 10:00 on Friday morning I got a call from Ginny on my bocce team. She sounded very upset. It took me a while to figure out that our game against the Pistons had been canceled.

Alex died suddenly last night!

It seemed that he had been walking on the path near his apartment when he fell and hit his head. He was dead when the security guard found him.

This news was a real shock and I sat down abruptly. It made me very sad to have lost another good friend. He was very funny and kind, always helpful to everyone.

The more I thought about it, the stranger it

seemed. Alex always went to balance class and was a star student. He had played brilliantly in the bocce game yesterday and showed no sign of any problems.

When I told the children that Alex had died, they couldn't believe it. Jeff said, "He seemed fine when we saw him."

Jane agreed, "That's so sad – he was really nice."

"Yes, he was pretty funny when he talked about your bocce throw," Roger added. I was happy that they had fun with Alex at the game but a little annoyed that they had been laughing at me. But I try not to stay angry at the dead, so I let Roger's comment pass.

I pointed out that Alex and Anita were both expert bocce players and team captains. I told them about Joan, who had died unexpectedly last year, and said I thought all three deaths might be suspicious. Perhaps Anita, Alex and Joan had all been killed by someone on a bocce team who wanted to win.

They all looked at me somewhat doubtfully.

Jeff asked, "Do you know if Joan even played bocce?"

"Do you think that winning bocce games is that important?" Roger asked.

They seemed to think by the time you are old enough to live in Golden Oaks you should have learned sportsmanship. They are still very innocent.

I said, "Well I personally would not go to that much effort to win, but this is the only clue we have so far. It's important to keep an open mind and examine all the facts."

"Let's start by trying to see why someone might want to kill bocce players," I suggested.

They still looked doubtful. But Jeff finally agreed, "OK, maybe that nurse lady we see all the time at the court is just kind of crazy and a really bad sport, so she might have done it."

"Since she was a nurse she could give shots of poison," Jane offered.

"Or maybe give them poisoned candy or cake," Roger added.

"What about using carbon monoxide?" I suggested. They smiled and exchanged glances, but I knew that examining all possibilities helps develop critical thinking. Teaching moments like these are invaluable – it is very important for grandparents to pass on knowledge to the younger generation.

I was very impressed when Jane pointed out, "But Alex fell – how could she have killed him?"

After a thoughtful pause Jeff suggested, "Maybe she pushed him."

"Or threw something at him," added Roger, "maybe a bocce ball."

They discounted my thought that he might have been struck by a well-hit golf ball. I admitted that scenario was unlikely but stressed the need for us to consider all angles in such a complex case.

We agreed that Ted and Carol should be looked at as possible suspects although, for some reason, the children seemed a little doubtful about Carol's involvement.

After our brainstorming session we made a list of possibilities:

1 This is all coincidental and, as Mr. Andrews said, older people sometimes die suddenly or have a fatal fall.
2 Someone is murdering people at Golden Oaks.

We made a list of suspects:
1 Carol (my number one suspect who could be poisoning people with injections. As a former nurse she might have access to drugs)

2. Ted (super competitive and obnoxious)
3. Another bocce player
4. A disgruntled employee (The word disgruntled is often used to explain mass shootings; it seems to fit nicely in this case and I like the way it sounds.)

This still leaves a lot of possibilities. But as I pointed out to the kids, it's important to keep an open mind. A good starting point would be to narrow down the possible motives and methods.

We decided to start a serious investigation. Jane thought that I would need to be very careful and that there could be some danger especially after they leave and I am alone in the apartment.

Roger said, "Let's make a trap near your front door. If someone is killing bocce players they might try to attack you." He is very creative and said he would make plans and send them to me so I could set up the trap.

Jeff pointed out that so far only good bocce players have been killed so I would probably be safe – he is very realistic.

Then Jane said, "Grandma is not a great player but she's not terrible. The danger is that the killer might figure out that she is suspicious of them." Jane is both analytical and kind.

CHAPTER 10

On Friday I fixed breakfast for the kids. Jeff wanted my special toast (I'll try to remember to include the recipe in the back of the book). Roger had leftover pizza and Jane had yogurt and a waffle with chocolate chips. And of course I fixed a special green smoothie for all of us.

After breakfast Jane suggested that we should look around the bocce court and the garden for clues. "The boys can show us some of the things they learned in CSI camp." It makes me happy that she is always supportive of her brothers.

We looked at the path where Alex had fallen

and Jane pointed out that it was half way between the bocce court and the garden. I said that he may have been on his way to the bocce court for a quick practice or the garden to water his plants.

Roger said, "Let's start at the bocce court; maybe we'll find some clues." He paced off the length of the bocce court while Jeff examined all the bocce balls. No balls were missing and there was no sign of blood on any of them. Jane noticed that none of the bocce balls looked as though it had been recently washed.

"Now let's check for clues in the garden," Roger said. We walked to the community garden and found Anita's plot in the right-hand corner next to the shed; we admired her herbs and beautiful flowers.

"That's strange -- parts of her garden have weeds and some parts look like someone was just here," Jeff pointed out. "We need to find out who was in her garden recently."

Alex's garden was next to Anita's and was filled with tomatoes and basil. The tomatoes were growing wildly and I picked one for a salad. Jane questioned whether I should do this, but I assured her that Alex would have wanted us to enjoy one.

Jeff pointed to another garden and said, "Look at that one – it has flowers like the ones in Anita's garden." We looked at it carefully; it was very neat with stone walkways between rows of perfectly mulched plants. Not a weed was in sight. We checked the chart in the shed and found that the garden belonged to Ella.

"You better talk to her," Roger suggested.

Jeff agreed, "She might have seen something that could be a clue."

I had only seen Ella a few times but said I would try to speak to her soon. Jane said, "Just try to be friendly and casual." I was proud that all three children were developing such good investigative skills.

Before we left the community garden we pulled a few weeds in my garden and watered everything carefully. We picked some kale to make kale chips for a snack and some green beans to add to the salad.

By that time we were hungry and I made BLT sandwiches with Alex's tomato for lunch. The sandwiches were very tasty, but the kids were not excited by the kale chips. I thought Jane still did not fully approve of eating Alex's tomato.

In the afternoon we walked down the trail

to the tennis court. Lines for pickleball had recently been added to the court. The kids had never heard of pickleball so I explained that it's kind of a cross between badminton (or is it ping pong?) and tennis. A pickleball court is smaller than a tennis court so there isn't much running and it's supposed to be easier for older people.

I told them that Lynn and I sometimes play pickleball after supper when it isn't too hot. She is 86 years old and quite athletic, but neither of us hits the ball very far or runs very fast. We don't officially keep score but I'm always aware of who is hitting the best shots. Today's practice session will help improve the length of my volleys.

The kids wanted to play tennis today. I got the ball over the net about half the time but occasionally missed it completely. Roger said, "Keep your eye on the ball," and Jeff added, "Be sure to follow through with your swing."

I asked, "Isn't that what you told me to do in golf?"

Jane replied, "Yes, it's true for almost any sport."

I commented, "It is probably good advice for most things in life."

After a few practice swings, I could see improvement and thought that the ball went farther and straighter with each shot. I told them that I thought this would really help me when I play with Lynn next time. They encouraged me to use the backboard and practice if I want to improve even more. When I got a little out of breath, I sat on the bench to watch them play.

Later that afternoon we relaxed by painting on the patio outside my apartment. The children know that I am a serious artist and they seem to have inherited my love of painting; on every visit they suggest that we paint together. We did not discuss the case while we worked. I told them that focusing on the act of painting is a form of meditation. If they became concerned about how their painting looked, I reminded them that perfection is boring and sometimes the best things happen unexpectedly.

In spite of the fact that we did not talk about the investigation, all of their paintings contained a feeling of mystery – Roger's painting of a spider web with both spider and fly seemed to sum up the case nicely.

CHAPTER 11

The kids and I took a walk after supper. There was a bocce game in progress so we stopped to watch. The Tornados were playing the Devils in a very close game. As usual, Carol was sitting on the bench so I stood behind her and tried to glance over her shoulder at her notes. Her handwriting was hard to read so I had no idea what she was writing and didn't want to make my interest too obvious.

Lynn was having a particularly good game and scored about four points while we were watching. She is very competitive but always willing to help other players no matter which team they are on.

Most of the players were certainly having fun. They cheered for their team but also cheered if a member of the other team made a particularly good shot. It was hard to believe that one of them could be so competitive that they would kill anyone.

I thought back to the other day when we played the Sonics. The Sonics are an extremely competitive team and Ted, their captain, seems determined to win the championship. I never heard him make a positive remark about anything. As a matter of fact, he seems angry every time I see him on the bocce court or around campus.

After the game we walked over to Dora's Ice Creamery. Roger likes the lemon sherbet and Jane and Jeff had chocolate cones. I had a hot fudge sundae.

We stayed up late playing board games and went to bed about 10:30. I wanted to make it a special evening because the children would be going home the next day. Their parents had completed their trip and would pick them up on the way back from the airport in the morning.

CHAPTER 12

We ate breakfast and had time for a quick game of golf before Gary and Elizabeth arrived to pick up the children. I was very happy that the ball soared at least seven feet on my first swing. My second swing missed the ball completely and Jeff reminded me to keep my head down and my eye on the ball.

Jane said, "It's so fun here and there is so much to do. How old do you have to be to move in?"

I replied, "You have to be 55 but most people are closer to 75 when they move here."

Jeff figured that their parents would be old enough to move here in about ten years. Roger said, "Then when we get old we can move in and we'll all have apartments near each other."

They promised to continue to help me solve this mystery after they get back to Ohio. It won't be easy because they don't have phones. I don't understand why people don't have landlines any more. They are a good way for children to make calls and stay in touch with their friends.

Jane said, "I think I'll get a phone in a few weeks because I need one when I start middle school. That way we can call or text you every day."

When Gary and Elizabeth arrived, we prepared a special salad for them using lettuce and vegetables from my garden. I added another tomato from Alex's garden and was pretty sure he would have approved.

Before they left I took Gary aside and hinted that a phone might be just the thing for a middle school student. I also remembered to tactfully suggest that the kids might be watching too many TV shows containing violence.

Chapter 13

After my family left I went to see Mr. Andrews again. This time I got right to the point and told him about Alex and my suspicion.

Mr. Andrews was quiet for a secybit then said, "My dear, you have to realize that falls are a common cause of death in older people. There's no reason to suspect foul play. I know you were involved in some kind of mystery a few years ago, my dear, but that doesn't mean anything sinister is happening at Golden Oaks."

We chatted for a few minutes but the conversation was going nowhere so I walked out of his office with quiet dignity and said, "I'll keep you posted, sweetie." As I closed the door I thought I heard him laughing.

You might have noticed that I reacted a little

when he called me "my dear." Often waitresses and salespeople call seniors "sweetie" and "honey" and sound patronizing, as though they are speaking to a very young child. And when people in management use these terms it's upsetting to me. It's like they think when your hair turns white your brain turns into marshmallows.

Or maybe I'm too sensitive. Maybe he couldn't remember my name. My uncle Frank called every woman "sweetheart" and meant no offence. And what about the young men who call each other "Dude"?

I am 85 years old and even though I have white hair my brain has not turned into marshmallows! Sometimes my grandchildren call me "flabby and forgetful" but they probably mean it as a compliment.

I also want to mention that I have solved several mysteries. Mr. Andrews was probably referring to one that happened three years ago on a painting trip to France. A valuable painting disappeared and an artist was killed. Clues in my paintings helped the police solve the mystery. The incident was on the evening news for days and my book, A Brush with Death, made the New York Times best seller list.

One reason I have been able to solve such difficult cases is that people are not threatened by me. I may give the erroneous impression that I am so involved in my painting that I am not paying attention. Some people think that all older people are hard of hearing. There is much to learn by sitting quietly and listening.

Have you noticed that some people direct conversation to the younger person? My father's doctor would ask me about my dad's symptoms and give instructions to me even after I tried to redirect the conversation to include my father.

Recently I was horrified when a waitress turned to my daughter-in-law and asked, "Does she want her hamburger rare?" "Did you just ask **her** how **I** want **my** food?" I demanded, striking a tone between snippy and haughty. I'm happy to report that the waitress seemed a little embarrassed.

That night as I fell asleep I became philosophical. Golden Oaks is not for everyone. My friend Josie talks about moving here but I fear she would be miserable. She is very judgmental and has no patience with people who do not agree with her. She's definitely not a rule follower. There are expectations here – not enforced but certainly understood.

Some people wait too long to make the move. If you are over 90 or in poor health it may become harder to find friends and activities.

I think that our personalities stay very much the same as we age. Basic traits may become even more pronounced. I have known Josie for many years and she has always been judgmental. Ted was probably angry even as a child. I of course have always been perfect. Our bodies may have changed, but we feel about the same inside at 85 as we did when we were 30 or maybe even when we were 12 years old.

Part Two

October 2019 – June 2021

Murder? A Memoir

CHAPTER 14

I apologize for jumping around a bit but it might be good to review the past year. Going back in time might help me figure out if there is really a problem to investigate.

Phyllis, Anita and I went out for lunch almost every Thursday during 2019 and early 2020. We picked a different restaurant each time and Anita drove. To tell the truth I don't like to drive, and Anita does so it works out well.

I remember that when we ate at The Irish Potato, Phyllis and Anita talked about their friend Joan Alexander who had died suddenly the week before. "I didn't know she was sick.

What happened?" I asked.

"It was very sudden." Anita replied. "Joan felt dizzy when we were in the garden and had to sit down on the ground. Ella was in her garden and she came over to see what was wrong. She gave Joan some water, and when that didn't help, I pressed the call button on my pendant. One of the nurses came out to check on Joan. Her blood pressure was very high so the nurse called an ambulance and Joan went to the hospital."

As I remember, Anita said that Joan stayed in the hospital overnight and died the next day. I hadn't known her well but was still very sorry to hear she had died. We talked about other friends who had been in the hospital then moved on to discussing the hospital itself. It is a place we all want to avoid.

Before long the subject of bocce came up, as it often does at Golden Oaks. Bocce is a big deal here – everybody of any importance is on a team. There are ten teams; several games are played every day throughout the summer. The court has a roof so we even play when it rains unless of course there is a thunderstorm.

Anita was excited that her team, the Golden Eagles, had won all their games so far this year.

She is team captain and an excellent player. "Can you believe that I am the high scorer!" she exclaimed.

I nodded politely but didn't comment because we were playing them soon and I knew we would beat them soundly. After all, I have been getting in top shape with the exercise classes. Many good players lack my physical ability and have significant physical challenges. One woman has both vision and memory problems but is able to follow her husband's directions and make excellent shots.

Reviewing my bocce career not only brings back pleasant memories, it may help me to understand more about the death of my friends and to see more clearly if anything suspicious occurred.

Bocce is thought about year-round in Golden Oaks. In February a meeting called "An Introduction to Bocce" tells newcomers about the game and encourages them to join a team. In the fall there is a luncheon where ribbons go to high scorers and a trophy to the best team. After the fall lunch there is a "talent" show put on by residents and staff. Like many shows in retirement communities, the talent is uneven and anyone can participate.

A few of the regulars from Zumba planned to put on a skit for the fall show based on our class and asked me to join them. I am quite shy and try to avoid the limelight whenever possible so I hesitated. But it sounded like fun and I was making an effort to become more social so I hesitantly agreed.

I remember that Alex, the head of the bocce league, introduced each act. The joke was that we were described as athletic, just coming off a tour of Europe and going to Rockefeller Center in a few weeks. Of course we were pathetic and it was supposed to be funny. There was a lot of laughter during the show and later I got compliments from some people and pitying looks from others.

In late February 2020 I went to the introductory meeting to find out more about bocce. I learned that players get a point if their ball is the closest one to a little yellow ball called a pallino. The team that reaches a score of 21 first wins. It sounded easy enough, so I decided to join as a sub.

After the meeting Fred (from Zumba) and Alex (the head of the whole bocce league) asked me to be on their team!

I was astounded and said that I had never

played bocce but was thinking of becoming a sub. Alex explained that his wife had died during the winter and shortly before her death she told him to ask me to join the team. He had never heard of me and I had never met his wife.

Why she wanted me on the team was a mystery to us all. My theory was that she thought the introduction at the fall talent show (which stressed our athletic ability) was true and I was just having a bad day during the skit. Anyway, it seemed to be fate, so I agreed.

Alex was very gracious but I suspected he was not too pleased at having me on the team. He and his wife were excellent and competitive bocce players – rumor had it they had a bocce court in their backyard before moving to Golden Oaks. But he had been a devoted husband for over 50 years and he said this was his wife's last request.

Alex offered to show me how to play bocce and we went to the court for a quick lesson. My shots veered wildly to the left and usually went several feet past the pallino, sometimes crashing into the wall at the end of the court. I quickly set a goal to become a mediocre player.

Alex very patiently explained how to roll the ball. He suggested using my left hand. This seemed to slow down the ball but it still veered to the left. He was an excellent teacher and encouraged me by saying if I kept practicing I might be able to meet my goal of becoming a mediocre player by the end of summer.

Chapter 15

In March of 2020 there was news of a strange new virus. Parts of China and Italy were locked down and there was fear that the virus might come here. People were concerned about possible shortages, so I went to ShopRite and bought enough food, toilet paper and other supplies to last for three weeks figuring that would be plenty.

By the end of March restaurants closed due to Covid-19 and our weekly lunches in town ended. Activities at Golden Oaks stopped. Exercise classes were discontinued. The upcoming bocce season was cancelled. Those of us in the apartments could no longer enter the main building. Masks were required even when walking around campus. We were social-distancing and I hadn't been anywhere in weeks.

April 2020 seemed unusually beautiful – the trees and flowers bloomed profusely. Or maybe it's always this lovely, and I'm just around more this year to notice it. Bonnie and I made a resolution to paint all the trees and buildings at Golden Oaks. She is a talented artist but her time to paint is limited because she is caring for her husband who cannot be left alone. An aide came for a few hours today so she had time for herself.

I love to paint. Before the pandemic I painted en plein air (that is French for painting outside in a pretty place) with a group of friends every Wednesday. They do not live at Golden Oaks so this gave us a good chance to see one another. We stopped painting when restaurants closed because we are also an eating group.

I want to clarify that I'm not a famous artist. You won't find my work in any of the big museums. But I sell paintings through an art gallery in New York City. I also sell internationally through my website and on Etsy. If you search Etsy you'll be able to see some of my paintings. And even if I don't become famous, it's a lot of fun and probably good for the brain. I'm pretty sure it helps with observational skills.

Painting certainly gave me something to do during the early spring of 2020. Of course I expected things to get back to normal after a few weeks. As social distancing dragged on and on, the frequency of my painting around campus slowed. What can you do with hundreds of paintings? Even with selling on Etsy, I had quite a collection. I started to paint over old paintings.

I try to exercise even though classes have been cancelled. The full loop around Golden Oaks is almost two miles and I walk it at least once a day. If it rains I pop an exercise DVD in the machine. At 7:30 I watch Wheel of Fortune and ride my exercise bike. I have been doing this for about forty years unless I am away. I am thinking of writing a letter to Pat and Vanna to let them know how much they have improved my health and my vocabulary.

One day on a morning walk I met a pleasant woman wearing a blue mask. We had a very friendly conversation and she said I was the first person she had spoken to in a week. We introduced ourselves. Her name is Annie and she is a former teacher. She lives up on the hill in Tree Tops and just loves her view and apartment but is a little bored because she hasn't been able to meet her neighbors.

I walked past Anita's place in The Meadows almost daily and waved in the general direction of her apartment. She watches people passing by and says she rates their walking skills. I thought she was joking until one day she called and described Clara as walking like a wind-up toy. Apparently most of the men walk with their hands clasped behind their backs.

After we had laughed at several people, she said, "Cate, do you know that you look down at the ground as you walk? It doesn't help your posture."

I remember being a little miffed. As I thought it over I realized she might have a point. Maybe since my fall I was looking at the ground in an attempt to avoid tripping. So the next day I kept my head high and looked straight ahead as I passed her apartment. After a week of doing this I realized that looking at the ground really wasn't necessary. I can see obstacles on the path even if I look straight ahead. Plus it felt good. Now I try to keep my head erect as I walk. Maybe it's my imagination but my double chin seems to be melting away.

Chapter 16

My neighborhood group formed during the pandemic. We were tired of social distancing and bored with spending so much time alone.

Almost every day you can find us talking in the backyard. We celebrate everybody's birthday. We use the grill by the guest house for barbecues. We often have impromptu pizza parties. Anyone is welcome to stop by, but the core group stays the same.

Phyllis and Lynn are the ringleaders in setting up our informal activities. I first met Lynn when she took an art class I taught years ago. One day I saw her at ShopRite shortly after she moved here. She said that she loved Golden Oaks and invited me to stop over and take a look; I was interested in downsizing so I decided to accept her offer.

Lynn has a lovely flower garden around her apartment and grows vegetables in the community garden. She's one who notices things in need of work around campus and is quick to make recommendations about almost anything if she thinks it could help someone.

I tend to be stubborn and resist suggestions but many of Lynn's ideas are good. The ability to make suggestions that don't annoy people is a useful skill and one I need to practice. Some of the things I suggest to my son and grandchildren are not accepted as promptly as I would like.

I invited Annie to join us and she was excited to meet a new group of people. She is a short, pretty woman who is very friendly and chatty. She is a good listener and makes people feel that she understands them. Consequently everyone likes her a great deal. But I've noticed that she says nothing about herself or her beliefs and it seems to me that we really don't know much about her.

Today Annie proudly showed us Biff, her seven month old puppy. Biff insisted on examining everyone before sitting by her feet. "He is a rescue, mostly poodle – I think I'll get his DNA tested to be sure. He is so sweet and I think he must be the smartest dog in the world. He seems to know my every thought."

Biff did not look like a poodle to me and I saw no sign of super intelligence but will try to keep an open mind.

Skoota Man often rolls by and joins the group. He is welcome everywhere around campus and knows what is going on before almost anyone else does.

My neighbor Kika joins us when she is home. She is 75 years old with short white hair and a cheerful expression. Her parents live in their own home about 50 miles away. Kika spends half her time there and has aides who are with them the rest of the time. She usually brings delicious homemade cake or cookies to our gatherings. She is a terrific bocce player, she has lovely gardens around her apartment and she is an excellent painter. I get exhausted just thinking about her.

Bonnie lives on the other side of the little golf course. She was born in Ireland and came to the US in her twenties but still has a bit of a brogue. She's very friendly and outgoing and often brings her guitar to our gatherings. Everybody loves to sing along with her. Well almost everyone – I don't sing but enjoy listening to the music. I tell myself that you can't be good at everything.

Sally stops by and interrupts our conversation. Today she opened by telling us about one of her two cats. "Mittens is the sweetest little thing, always following me around." Then we hear about great-granddaughter Tiffany who is in preschool "cute as a button and so bright." Then on to grandson Tom who is in graduate school at NYU "such a brilliant student." After a breath she brings us up to date on her sister-in-law who might move to Texas.

Sally is a non-stop talker and I think she gets nervous if there is any lull in conversation and feels she must fill the empty space. Usually after several minutes someone jumps in and changes the subject so I have no idea how long she would go on if uninterrupted.

Thomasina comes to our gatherings when she remembers them. She is a lot of fun and has a good sense of humor but a very poor memory. I try to remind her to join us but a few minutes later she seems to have forgotten. We worry if she should continue to live alone. Someone usually says, "Thank goodness her son comes over every day."

Some people complain that Golden Oaks is cliquey, but it seems to me that friendships form here much the way they do every place. Smaller groups develop around shared interests. I have friends who paint; Phyllis has friends who play cards. Some groups are focused on health issues; other groups talk politics, religion or gardening. Our friendly, informal neighborhood group has helped us all get through the social distancing of 2020.

CHAPTER 17

Thomasina isn't the only one with memory problems. Four years ago Dalia was a few minutes late to committee meetings; then she missed meetings completely; now she seldom leaves her apartment.

When I first moved here my neighbor Edna often forgot names. It was hard to watch her slip from forgetting names to getting lost around our rather small campus. Last year her son convinced her to move into Memory Care and I'm very pleased that she seems happier. Last week I saw her walking hand in hand with one of the men who lives there.

I don't think that I told you about my father. After Mom died 30 years ago my sister, brother and I were worried because Dad was becoming very forgetful. We talked him into moving to Golden Oaks because I lived nearby. He hated it at first and could never have managed without his next door neighbor Maryanne. She invited him for lunch every day and they had supper together in the main dining room every evening.

My father went into the nursing unit after a fall. A woman in a nearby room had serious dementia and did not recognize her family. Dad was upset because she often wandered into his room and took things.

She developed pneumonia and was taken to the hospital where she recovered. The nurse told me that this had happened at least three times over the past year. She said that if there are no written instructions the staff is required to do everything possible to prolong life.

While in the nursing unit my father got very confused. Maryanne urged me to have him discharged, saying he would improve in his own home. She was right. When he got home, he bounced back to his pleasantly confused state and was able to live alone for another year with her help.

I was a little concerned that she might be a gold digger and am embarrassed to admit that

I consulted a lawyer to set up a trust so that she would not gain access to his money. After Dad's death she adopted another man who lived nearby and needed her care. Maryanne and I had become friends and I had long since realized that her motivation was not financial. Some people are natural caregivers and seem happiest when they have someone to help.

Memory problems can run in families, so this is something that I have some concern about. I've developed a few memory tips that you might find helpful.

In meetings I look around the room and try to name everybody there. I become a little concerned if I don't recognize somebody or cannot remember their name when I see them in another location.

I keep a daily schedule on my phone and on a piece of paper on the kitchen counter. I write notes about this investigation on my phone (I need notes to remember my ideas). I don't write these notes on paper because I do not want anyone to see this information (although with my handwriting they probably could not read it). I shouldn't tell you this but at this point I have no idea who the killer is or what the motive is.

I try to help my grandchildren memorize things like their multiplication tables and spelling words by suggesting they sing or dance while they repeat the facts over and over. They usually just roll their eyes and pay very little attention.

The amount of valuable information that gets lost from generation to generation is frightening.

Chapter 18

In spite of the pandemic, people are still moving to Golden Oaks. Apparently the suburbs are a hot real-estate market because people are leaving New York City seeking the safety of open space. As a result, houses in this area sell very quickly for good prices. The former owners have to live somewhere, and some have come to Golden Oaks

Moving is hard any time. Moving to a retirement community during a pandemic must be extremely difficult because not only have activities been canceled, but new residents are asked to quarantine in their apartments for two weeks.

One warm day we set up chairs in my backyard to welcome Hazel to our neighborhood. She was wearing a stylish dress and an irritated look; her ash blond hair looked as though she had just left the beauty shop.

Phyllis asked, "How do you like your apartment?"

Hazel grumbled, "I guess I was spoiled by my lovely home – did you know I lived in Scarsdale? That is such a beautiful town. I only moved here to be near my son. My house was huge and this apartment is so small. I brought 20 beautiful paintings with me and there's only enough wall space for a few of them."

Annie spoke up, "I just moved here a few months ago and brought too much stuff with me but you can donate what you don't need to the Golden Oaks Store. Maintenance will even pick it up for you."

This started another round of complaints from Hazel. "The staff sometimes takes an hour to come to help me with something in my apartment." She went on, "My artwork is valuable, and I would only donate it where it would be appreciated. I don't think anyone here understands art – maybe a museum might be a possibility."

She continued, "I have beautiful china and glassware and there is almost no shelf space in the kitchen. And the bedroom closet is so small that there is no place to put all my lovely clothes. Do they have many dressy events here? I hope so – I have some amazing formal dresses."

I glanced at the jeans and tee shirt that are my outfit for almost every occasion and decided to try another subject. "Do you have family in the area?"

"I'm glad you asked," she grumbled. She then proceeded to describe her family in detail. Her brilliant son lives nearby with his shrewish wife. When she got down to her great grandson "He's a real genius – can you believe he reads on a 5th grade level? And he's only seven years old?" I excused myself to get another brownie. I don't understand why so many people are so focused on their grandchildren.

Hazel is not the only one with complaints. When Gloria stops by our gatherings she reviews all her aches and pains. "There was too much garlic in the sauce on the salmon the other day and my stomach still has not recovered." When there is no reaction to this statement she continues, "My sciatica is really bad today. I think this weather makes it worse."

Gloria pulls up her sleeve and points to a small spot on her arm. She asks, "Does this look serious to you, Betty?"

"No, I think it is just a freckle. You showed it to me last week and it hasn't changed," Betty, a retired nurse, replied patiently.

Many residents share Gloria's focus on health problems. It seems to me that focusing on people and activities you love is a better plan. I think that constant worry about health is counterproductive and may actually increase pain.

When I was thinking of moving to Golden Oaks my son urged me to consider a condo. He was concerned that the atmosphere of a retirement complex could accelerate my aging process. Now we agree that having contact with a variety of people and taking part in the activities at Golden Oaks has helped with the challenges of 2020. It's probably good to decide before your children suggest that you might not be able to manage your home. If Gary had pushed Golden Oaks I would have resisted.

CHAPTER 19

Phyllis and Bonnie threw a surprise birthday party for me in May of 2020. Most of the gang was there, but Anita stayed home because her headaches had gotten worse and she was uncomfortable in a group – even outdoors with everyone wearing masks. Hazel wasn't there; I didn't ask if she had been invited. Someone said Gloria's birthday is next week and suggested we make a special get-well birthday card for her birthday. Social distancing is not making us more tolerant.

Golden Oaks set up a huge tent with tables and chairs so we could play card games outside and stay socially distanced. Phyllis and I went to play Rummikub on Thursday. I avoid playing with people who take the game seriously. I really enjoy the first hour but must have a short attention span because by the second hour I lose interest and can't wait to go home. This can be a problem because Phyllis won't leave until she wins at least one game.

Ted and Agnes and another couple were playing bridge at a table on the other side of the tent. Ted's voice carried and he ridiculed the other players, including Agnes. If he didn't like a bid he barked, "Pay attention! You're acting like a nitwit."

We laughed when we heard Ted say, "Speak up, can't you?" every few minutes. Ted insists his hearing is good "maybe a little wax in the ears." According to Phyllis, he is driving his wife to distraction because he won't have a hearing test and would never consider hearing aids. Ted does have a point about hearing aids. Some people don't hear well even with them. Occasionally someone's aid makes a screechy noise, which is aggravating to the wearer and startles people nearby.

Many people at Golden Oaks have some hearing loss and generally handle it with good humor. Occasionally I overhear conflicting conversations:

Samantha, "How are you feeling today,

Sally?"

Sally, "No I don't think it's going to rain today."

Samantha, "I'm glad you are feeling better. Do you think it will rain?"

Sometimes the frustration shows. Saturday night movies are run by volunteers who must find it difficult to adjust the sound. Some people complain, "I can't hear a thing. Turn up the volume, can't you?" Others just as forcefully say, "Turn it down – it hurts my ears".

My neighbor Bill is completely deaf. We communicate through **Visual Voice,** an app that translates speech into large print text. Once he asked if I was going to the garden. I spoke into my phone and handed it to him. Bill read my message, laughed and said, "Of course you are, but are you going to the garden?" **Visual Voice** had changed "I am considering it" to "I am considered a nut."

Maybe technology will be able to help before long. At a party at Bonnie's last year, her sister-in-law proudly showed me her new hearing aids, which she said are the latest design. They are connected to Bluetooth, so phone calls go directly to the hearing aid. That day the aid was set for "group" because she wanted to hear everyone, but she can make a change on her cell phone and focus on a single speaker at a meeting.

Chapter 20

Our swimming pool opened in June! I think we are the only retirement complex in the state to open their pool in 2020. We can't have guests and are expected to socially distance and to wear masks when not in the water. The restrictions are a nuisance but having some place to go and people to see is a joy!

The tables and chairs grouped around the pool are shaded by tall trees, and flowers bloom everywhere. There is an umbrella at each table making this a cool, peaceful place to relax on a hot day.

July 5th was a very hot day. The pool was scheduled to open at 12:00 but was closed when I arrived about 12:45. I called the receptionist who thought it might be closed for the holiday. I was quite annoyed and telephoned Lynn, who has a real knack for getting things done. She made a few calls and the pool opened at 1:00.

I go to the pool almost every day and am surprised that not many residents take advantage of it – usually the same seven or eight people are there. I don't remember ever seeing Anita or Alex at the pool in 2020.

One afternoon Phyllis, Lynn and Skoota Man were in the pool when I arrived. It's the perfect place to splash around and chat – we don't need masks in the water. Kika was keeping her hair dry by floating with those plastic "noodles". Cindy joined us and started her exercise routine. She said that the heated salt water is wonderful therapy; I agreed and commented that the physical therapist told me that exercising in a pool was the best possible therapy for my shoulder.

As I was floating quietly the peace was disturbed by the sound of mowing machines. Suddenly there was a loud crash – I thought the lawnmower had bumped into something. I turned around and there was Hanzie who had cannonballed into the water and was laughing at my reaction.

He normally sits in the sun and reads and usually enters the pool in a much more dignified manner. Last year he suggested that we climb the fence one day when the pool was late opening. I'm not sure he would actually try this but you never know.

A few people are serious swimmers. Lynn and Joe swim laps, of course at different times because the six foot rule applies. Anna tries to swim one lap for each year of her life, but as she approaches her 79th birthday it has become more difficult.

Ted usually arrives at the pool around 2:00. He complains to the lifeguard about something then carefully walks down the stairs and barrels down a lane, scattering any residents in his path. After two laps he gets out of the pool and falls asleep in the sun.

Did I mention that Ted wears a speedo? It always is a surprise to see a paunchy 80 year old man with toothpick thin legs flash his speedo and then strut into the pool. Strut is too strong a word but I'm sure that is his intent.

My bathing attire is at the opposite end as I wear long sleeved rash guards. I had never heard of them until a few years ago but they are shirts with SPF 50 protection designed to prevent sunburn.

When I was in college we sat in the sun, spread baby oil all over ourselves and used reflectors to make sure that our faces got a good tan. At the time it seemed like a good plan even though my skin peeled off in long strips a few days after each tanning session.

Now I go to the dermatologist every six months. This year it seemed weird to be naked except for my mask. I asked the dermatologist if she thought this was kinky but she wasn't amused. On every visit I point out a few new spots to the dermatologist. She looks at them and then says, "That's just another barnacle on the sea of life." At first I thought this was clever but after hearing this phrase every six months for 10 years I'm a little tired of it.

Today she looks very carefully at my leg. "Have you had this spot for a long time?"

"I was here just six months ago so the spot must be pretty new," I reply as I put on my glasses and squint at my leg. That spot looks about the same as all the others to me.

"It needs to come off and be biopsied." Then the assistant takes a photo of the spot in question and the Doc removes it. Sometimes it is a basal cell but often nothing is wrong.

"See you in six months," she says.

"Do you think I still need to come that often?" I ask.

"Yes," she says, "These things can grow quickly and you don't want surgery later, do you?"

I accepted another appointment but am hoping that when her daughter graduates from college next year she may not be so insistent on seeing me.

CHAPTER 21

Social distancing remained in full swing and by October I had progressed to painting fall scenes. The orange and red colors of the leaves in rural New York make for vibrant paintings and the crisp air is still comfortable.

Politics caused considerable commotion, making it hard to really talk to each other. Some residents were still upset about Trump's impeachment in January. They were very happy with the progress he has made in spite of the "witch hunts" against him.

Other residents complained about his decisions and his handling of the pandemic. Lynn, a lifelong Republican, was upset by

Trump's actions and his way of talking. She sadly told me about arguments with friends who were outraged if she questioned any of his decisions.

There was ongoing debate about whether there really is a pandemic. Arguments erupted about the requirements for social distancing and mask wearing.

As the 2020 election neared, tempers sometimes flared. Ronald wore a MAGA hat all the time – he probably slept in it but I certainly would not want to find out. He had Trump signs on his car and a large Trump poster filling his front window. Someone filed a complaint to the council about his signs. After much debate it was decided that residents could wear what they please and have signs on their cars, but no political signs were permitted on apartment buildings or grounds. The next day Ronald's window sign came down, but he added two more signs to his car.

I can't say that people were satisfied by the council's decision because the snide remarks and dirty looks continued.

Families were affected by the political climate. Beverly told me that she and her husband watched the news every day in stony silence. She added sadly, "He was always conservative but up until this year we could at least discuss things." Several other friends almost stopped talking to their siblings because simple conversations turned into violent disagreements.

Politics has also divided the religious community. Golden Oaks was originally founded by the Methodist Church, and quite a few former ministers of all faiths live here. Some showed their support for Trump's pro-life policies with bumper stickers and signs.

On the other hand my neighbor, a former Episcopalian priest, was horrified by Donald Trump and became incensed when he thought of him. We had many interesting discussions of politics both in the US and in Canada. I am not religious and probably would have not become friends with Bill had he not been my neighbor. Last year his family talked him into moving near them in Canada. I miss him and hope he has avoided the worst of the pandemic and the political tension here.

In October, talk at Golden Oaks turned to the upcoming election. I was glad to vote by mail and not happy when Hazel announced, "Voting by mail is a scam. You might just as well throw your vote in the trash." I was very hopeful that the temperature of politics would begin to lessen after the election.

We talked about New Jersey's recent law for assisted dying. As you would expect, everyone had a different opinion. I gave my doctor a form stating that I do not want to be resuscitated or put on a ventilator, but she refused to sign it, saying I am too healthy. I am not satisfied with her response and may look for another doctor.

Assisted dying is a very complicated subject indeed. Years ago my father gave money to the Hemlock Society, which supports assisted suicide. But as he got older he retained a strong will to live and would never have considered anything to shorten his life.

By November Phyllis, Anita and I were desperate to get out. It was Phyllis's birthday and we wanted to celebrate. We decided to eat at The Ribald Raisin, a restaurant with outdoor seating and a fire pit in the center of each table. It was the first time we had gone anywhere in months and we were very excited. Anita was feeling much better and was willing to take a chance as long as we could eat outside.

We passed a group of people waving "Stop the Steal" signs and shouting. They sounded very angry, and I could feel my own anger welling up in response. Anita tooted the horn; she and Phyllis gave them a thumb-up and, from the safety of the back seat, I gave them the finger.

We had a delicious meal at the Ribald Raisin with no mention of politics. Phyllis, Anita and I are aware of our political differences but seldom discuss them. Probably if I had moved into Golden Oaks this year I might have decided we have nothing in common and avoided them. This would have been a shame because they are lots of fun and other than politics we agree on most subjects.

My reaction to the protesters surprised me; I had never given anyone the finger before. I thought back to my friend Martha, a very dignified lady, who broke the middle finger of her left hand when she hit it on the top of the car window during a disagreement with a passing driver. At the time I was amused and surprised at her story, but she may have been my inspiration. Anger can sometimes lead even the most civil of us in dangerous directions.

Chapter 22

A few days later, during my weekly phone call with Gary, I mentioned I had eaten at The Ribald Raisin. There was a moment of silence; then he said, "You did **WHAT**?" He was not appeased by my explanation of outdoor seating and fire pits.

The following week Elizabeth invited me to visit them in Ohio. Gary did not think I should take a plane and offered to come get me – driving that distance is way past my comfort zone so I gratefully accepted his offer.

I had a wonderful time and was happy I could stay for Jane's 11th birthday. Elizabeth had set up a classroom in the basement where she taught Jane, Jeff and Roger plus three other children. This kind of group is called a pod and they were on a hybrid schedule; it's too complicated to explain.

Toward the end of my visit, I asked my grandchildren to give me a haircut. Jane offered to color my hair pink or purple and assured me the powder would wash out if I didn't like the color. I was a little nervous about this idea so she offered to give me a manicure instead, using a different color for each nail. I was very pleased with the results of my makeover. The haircut got compliments upon my return home.

Life went on at Golden Oaks without me. I got occasional phone calls and texts from friends back home. People remained in their own apartments and all activities were still cancelled due to the pandemic. Golden Oaks sent a weekly email update during the pandemic. Several people in the health unit died of Covid-19 but no one living in independent housing had tested positive for Covid.

Everyone was horrified by the storming of the capitol on January 6th. I hoped that our mutual anguish over this event would finally help bring the country together.

In mid-January Golden Oaks offered vaccines to all interested residents. At first I was a little hesitant (my uncle had developed serious symptoms after a swine flu vaccination in the 70s) but decided that getting vaccinated was the best plan. Gary drove me back to Golden Oaks in time for my first shot and I'm happy to report that I had no adverse reaction.

Soon after my return to Golden Oaks in January 2021, winter arrived in full force and it snowed heavily almost every day. Almost three feet of snow fell in one day, and I worried that the birds would starve.

Bird feeders are discouraged here, because an occasional bear leaves the woods to walk around campus. I figured that no self-respecting bear would wake up in this storm, so I threw birdseed out the sliding glass doors of my patio. The birds quickly discovered the seeds and waited in the pine tree nearby, swooping out almost as soon as I tossed the seed. A deer stopped by and ate some seed, so I added carrots and apples for him.

I like to paint pictures of snow. In other years friends and I would go to a park to paint if the temperature warmed up and the snow was still deep. But this year my car was completely snowed in, so I painted snow scenes looking out my windows. Kika and I walked through the snow to paint a view of the gazebo. Her painting was pretty enough to be a Christmas card.

On a mild day in late January Lynn and I went snowshoeing. I had only snowshoed a few times and that was several years ago. It took me a while to figure out how to fasten the snowshoes to my boots. Once we got started it was a lot of fun. We walked across the small golf course and around the gazebo. But snowshoeing seemed harder than I remembered – before long we grew tired and headed back home. The tiredness was undoubtedly due to the heavy snow and not the extra years.

One afternoon Kika, Betty and I made snowmen using carrot noses and our best scarfs and hats. We felt like little kids again and it reminded me of last year when Kika's three year old grandson Zippy came to visit. During a sudden shower he went out to play in the rain and Kika, Betty and I joined him, dancing barefoot and singing in the rain.

Kika took photos of our snowmen and submitted them to the Acorn, the monthly newsletter at Golden Oaks. When the Acorn appeared our snowmen did not seem nearly as impressive as they had the day we made them.

Phyllis revived the idea of sledding but the snow was too deep and the dining room was closed so she could not borrow trays to use as sleds. Maybe we will try again next year.

Winter gave way to early spring of 2021. Bonnie and I resumed painting around campus but our hearts weren't in it. She painted small rocks with inspirational sayings and lovely pictures on them and placed them around campus or gave them as gifts to friends and new residents.

By May the pandemic seemed to be retreating. Golden Oaks was coming back to life and exercise classes resumed in early June. Phyllis, Anita and I made plans for our first meal in town in over a year. On a warm July day we went for lunch on the patio of an upscale restaurant on the outskirts of town.

Part Three

Late July 2021

CHAPTER 23

After the children returned to their home in Ohio in late July, I turned my full attention to solving these mysterious deaths. It was clear that Anita, Alex and Joan had died under unexplained circumstances. I thought Carol and Ted were the most likely suspects; it seemed to me that the children had some doubt about Carol but they are very young and may not appreciate all the small details.

Before they left, we had agreed that I should interview both Carol and Ted. Jane cautioned, "Grandma, you must be very casual. If they get suspicious you might be in danger."

Jeff reminded me that I should also talk to

Ella. She spent time in the garden with Anita and might have seen something significant.

I was a little nervous about talking to possible murderers. To delay interviewing them I made a simple chart showing what the victims have in common.

Victim	Trump	Bocce	Garden
Anita	Yes	Yes	Yes
Alex	Yes	Yes	Yes
Joan	?	?	Yes
?			

You will notice that under the **Victims** column there is a question mark (?) in the last row. It is possible that I may discover more victims as this case continues.

My chart shows that both Alex and Anita were Trump supporters, but I do not know Joan's political leanings. Could politics be a motive for murder? Were people as angry about politics at the time of Joan's death as they are now?

The depth of my own political feeling was becoming clear to me as I tried to solve this mystery. I admit that I sometimes want to shake neighbors who talk about their love for Donald Trump and their wish to overturn the election. But could anger turn to murder?

If politics was the motive, half of the residents at Golden Oaks, including me, would have to be considered suspects. Sure there was a lot of disagreement and some anger about our political views, but I did not think it had reached the murderous stage. In fact, the only incident that I am aware of that bordered on violence involved me – could giving Trump supporters the finger be considered violent? In any case I can assure you that I am not the killer.

Chapter 24

Even though my chart was useful, I saw a need for more sophisticated technology to sift through clues. Although I use a computer to sell paintings on my website and on Etsy, my tech experience is strictly seat-of-the-pants. I never look at user manuals but will occasionally ask someone who seems knowledgeable for help.

Jane used the app **Paint-all** to create a beautiful moonlit scene and I asked her to show me how to use the app. She was very gracious and patient but I still find it confusing.

I often call my sister in Chicago for tech support. Years ago we wrote a computer program to help teachers prepare lessons for children in special education. To tell the truth, my sister did most of the computing and I tested it. I also went to schools to provide customer support. I never enjoyed teaching groups of teachers about the program. To discourage requests for support, we charged $100 an hour, which seemed like a very large amount to us in those days.

Golden Oaks has a computer group that meets monthly. Meetings were discontinued during the pandemic but had started again. I knew I needed training to bring my computer skills up to date and thought of going to the next meeting to ask for help. Then I remembered that during the only meeting I had attended, members focused on problems with their own computers. Probably none of them had considered using technology in a criminal investigation. I also feared my questions might call attention to this case and possibly increase my danger.

Quite a few residents are "technologically challenged" and seem proud of it. They have no interest in getting a computer or a smartphone. Every time I visit Frank and Doris, he says that he has not touched a computer since he retired 20 years ago, because he had to use one every day at work and was tired of them. Once in a while he will ask his son to send an email for him.

Until I could find a good resource for using tech in my investigation, I decided to make another chart highlighting the suspects, their interests and possible motives:

Suspect	Bocce	Garden	Politics
Carol	Yes	?	yes
Ted	Yes	?	?
?			
?			

As this chart shows, my two suspects (Carol and Ted) were both involved with bocce. You will notice question marks (?) in the last two rows in case I find other suspects as I continue the investigation.

After a close study of both charts, I decided to begin by focusing on the role bocce might play in this mystery. Alex and Anita were team captains and high scorers. What about Joan? Did she play bocce? Was she a high scorer or a team captain? Could she have been seen as a threat by another player?

In an attempt to find out more about Joan, I asked five friends to join me for supper in the pub. I picked people who play bocce and have lived here for at least four years. They should certainly have some information about Joan.

This Friday the special was scallops – one of my favorites. After the wine was served, I casually asked, "Do you remember Joan Alexander? She died last year and I think she played bocce."

Kika said, "Sure. She was that tall lady with light brown hair who lived up on the hill."

Lynn said, "No, I don't think she died. She's chubby and lives in Aspen. I still see her in the garden a lot."

Betty said, "The Joan I'm thinking of was a really good knitter and she got around using a walker."

Kika said, "No, you're thinking of Joan Pope – she is in the bell choir. This Joan was in the book club and used a cane, not a walker."

Phyllis said, "Speaking of books, I just started reading a good one by Danielle Steel."

Betty said, "Those books are a waste of time. You should be reading something like Caste. It's all about the problems facing the country."

Lynn said, "Give me a good mystery any day," and I had to agree.

From there we started talking about books. Then we moved on to discussing food and recipes and Joan Alexander was forgotten.

As I walked home I realized I didn't gain any information about Joan. Nevertheless I was grateful for a good time and for good friends, and very happy that life in Golden Oaks seemed to be getting back to normal.

Chapter 25

The next day I decided to put thoughts of Joan aside for a while and focus on Alex's death. When the security guard found his body, Alex was midway between his two favorite places: the bocce court and his garden. Apparently, he had gone for a walk after supper and fell, hitting his head on a rock.

Or maybe he didn't fall; perhaps he was pushed; maybe a rock or bocce ball had been thrown at him. The children thought if the weapon had been a bocce ball the killer might have removed it. We had examined the bocce court before they left last week and did not find anything suspicious. All the bocce balls were at the court and there was no sign of blood on any of them.

I decided to start my formal investigation by

having a chat with Carol. She was my prime suspect because she spent so much time at the bocce court, watching all the games and taking notes.

Carol looks harmless enough. But on the other hand she seemed very opinionated and appeared annoyed if her statements about health were questioned. She also seemed to be obsessed with bocce. Was she even on a team? Why on earth was she so interested in the games and the players?

So Friday after aerobics class, I casually followed Carol out of the room. I knew she lived up on the hill, so I figured if I walked with her it would give plenty of time to have a casual but probing chat.

I wasn't quite sure how to open the conversation. "Have you killed anybody recently?" didn't seem like a good opening.

I decided to be more low-key and explained, "I sometimes take the scenic walk home after class just to get a little more exercise. This walk up the hill is the perfect distance."

Since I didn't know Carol very well, I asked, "Where did you live before you moved to Golden Oaks?"

She replied that she was from Nebraska and

moved here because her daughter lived about five miles away and she was eager to see her three grandchildren more often. They are about the ages of Jane, Jeff and Roger, and we shared a few stories about our grandchildren.

She asked, "Did you know that I am a former nurse?" I tried to keep a straight face because she mentions her nursing career in every conversation.

She went on to say, "I worked in a NICU with premature babies. I just love children and it was such a rewarding job." I knew that NICU stands for neonatal intensive care unit and was impressed by her concern for the babies.

As we approached her apartment, I casually said, "I have a bocce game this afternoon and I noticed you at the court fairly often. What team are you on?"

I suspected she didn't play but wanted to keep her talking.

She replied, "No, I'm not on a team and I've never played bocce but I'm thinking of joining a team next year. I took a few lessons on Saturdays with Skoota Man and Fern and learned a lot."

She grew more animated as she said, "The reason I go to the games is because I am writing an article for a nursing magazine about the benefits of even mild exercise."

She went on to say, "Did you know that simple and smooth movements of your arm can improve the health of your joints and lessen the chance of arthritis? I'm talking about the kind of moves bocce players make when they roll the ball. I also think that competition somehow adds to the beneficial effect, and I'm trying to determine how this works."

She added, "After I analyze how players roll the ball, I'll interview them to see how their attitude affects the outcome. Maybe competitive players have better bocce scores and less joint pain."

I said, "Wow, maybe that explains why my shoulder is improving so quickly now." I told her the story of how I broke my shoulder and said that it seemed to be improving more with bocce and exercise classes than it had with physical therapy.

Carol said, "That is very interesting and could certainly be the case. I'd like to include your experience in my article if it's OK with you."

I was honored and happy to agree. About that time we reached her apartment and said goodbye. I said, "Please let me know when you finish the article. I'd love to read it."

I walked back to my own apartment thinking about our conversation.

Could Carol have pushed Alex? She is petite and he was a big guy; it would have been hard for her to knock him over unless she caught him completely off guard. Could she have thrown a rock – or bocce ball – accurately and hard? It's possible but not likely.

What would be her motive for killing Alex? Carol doesn't play bocce so she probably would not care who won any of the games. She claimed to be writing an article about the health benefits of bocce. Killing one of the best players would not help prove her theory that playing bocce is good for your health. It's hard to see how Alex's death would affect her in any way.

At this point I thought I could rule out Carol as the killer. I may not have mentioned that I worked as a social worker and pride myself on my skill in assessing people. Like many people here, I have had several careers and interests through the years.

CHAPTER 26

I decided to look more closely at Ted, our other suspect. He definitely wants his team, the Sonics, to win the championship. During our game I had noticed that Ted seemed to be very focused on Alex's technique and was upset that Alex was such a skillful player. He had muttered something about the odds changing. What did he mean by that? I also overheard Ted complaining about the way Alex handled the job of league president.

It would appear that Ted may have had a motive.

I turned my attention from motive to method. It seemed possible that Alex's fall might have been caused by a push or being hit by a rock. Ted is definitely an angry guy with a short fuse — could he have done this after an angry discussion with Alex? He certainly is big enough and strong enough to have given Alex a shove that would knock him over. And judging from Ted's skill with a bocce ball, it seemed that he could probably throw accurately.

I needed to question Ted. I was a little nervous about approaching him because he is quite intimidating even under the best of circumstances.

I called Gary later that day and asked to speak to the kids. I had only a few minutes before going to my art group, so I got right to the point; "I'm getting ready to talk to Ted tomorrow. Do you remember him? He was at the pool when you were here — he makes me a little nervous. Do you have any ideas about how I should talk to him?"

"Do you even know for sure if Ted was in town when Alex was killed?" Jeff asked.

"Remember when we talked to Skoota Man at the pool? I think he said Ted would go to Maine soon," Roger added. It occurred to me that Skoota Man knows a lot about what is going on around campus and I made a mental note to think more about what he might know and the role he may have played.

Jane suggested, "Maybe someone who works there knows where Ted was. It's important to find this out before you talk to him. But be very careful when you see him. I think he could be dangerous."

I decided to talk to Margaret, our receptionist. Margaret has worked at Golden Oaks for 25 years and knows all the residents by name and seems to like everybody. She also has a terrific memory.

Margaret never gives out personal information about people and she never gossips. I would have to approach her carefully. I decided it would probably make more sense for me to ask about Ted's wife, Agnes, than about Ted.

"Hi Margaret," I said casually. "I love the colors in your blouse." (This was true as her blouse really was pretty.) Then I swung into my story, "I've been trying to contact Agnes about the dining committee and haven't been able to get in touch with her. Do you know if they're out of town?"

"Yes," she said, "I do believe that they are away for a while."

"I tried to call her last week also," I lied.

"Were they away then too?"

Margaret said she thought that they left sometime on Monday last week.

So this seems to eliminate both my prime bocce suspects. Carol has no motive and Ted was out of town that week.

Of course, there are still another 40 bocce players who could have been involved but it was beginning to seem less likely that bocce was the motive. As Roger said, is bocce really a reason to kill someone?

Chapter 27

I was on my way out the door for an evening walk when the phone rang. I did not recognize the number so I ignored it. I do not need an extended warranty for my car which has over 100,000 miles.

I had only gone a few steps when I heard a loud whistle. It was Bonnie. "Hey Cate, wait up! I'll walk with you." She jogged up the hill and wasn't even slightly winded when she reached me. The sun was starting to set, and the pink and gold clouds grew brighter by the minute. It was beautiful and we decided to paint a series of sunsets from my patio. I commented sadly, "The forest fires out west are making the sunsets really bright." Bonnie agreed, "I sure don't miss 2020 but 2021 has a few problems too."

I played the answering machine when I got home, and it was Jane! "Hey Grandma, it's me! I just got my own phone! Give me a call when you have a chance."

I called her immediately and put the number in my contacts file so I would know who it was next time she called. (See, I told you I was good with technology.)

"Congratulations, Jane!" I said, "When did you get the phone?"

"Mom and Dad gave it to me yesterday. They thought it was a good idea for me to have a phone before I start middle school in two weeks. All my friends have them. Now I can talk to them."

"That's wonderful!" I exclaimed "Now you can keep up with everything in middle school. And it will help you to work on this case!"

"So Grandma, speaking of the case, is there any news?" she asked. She put the phone on speaker. Luckily both Jeff and Roger were with her, so we could all brainstorm.

I thanked them for suggesting that Ted might have been out of town when Alex died, and I told them that Margaret had verified this.

"I guess we can be sure that he is not the killer," Roger said a little sadly.

Then I told them about my conversation with Carol. I said, "Her story makes sense to me, and I don't think she killed anyone." They had been doubtful that she was the killer and I could almost picture them rolling their eyes and saying, "I told you so."

I quickly added, "Let me send you some charts that I made. They list some things that the victims had in common. Maybe you can look at them and see something that I haven't figured out yet."

We agreed that politics is not a likely motive. I pointed out that if politics was the motive, I would be the prime suspect. They assured me that they did not consider me to be a murderer.

Roger said, "Okay, Grand. We will be glad to look at the charts for you! I'm glad we could get back on the case! We'll call you in a few days."

Jeff said, "I think you need to keep looking around the garden. There might be a lot of clues there."

Jane reminded me, "Have you talked to Ella yet? We need to know if she saw something that can help us."

As soon as I got off the phone I emailed charts to the kids. They all have their own email, so they can each have a chart to study. I was glad to have their help again in trying to figure out what was going on.

CHAPTER 28

My investigation has ruled out bocce and politics as possible motives. My charts show that Joan, Anita and Alex were all gardeners.

The children had reminded me that the garden could contain valuable clues and that Ella might have important information. Now it seems important to consider what role gardening may have played in these mysterious deaths.

What would be a motive for killing gardeners? Are some plants really that valuable?

Anita was making elixirs from her herbs to lessen her headaches. She also grew prize irises and was proud to be part of an organization dedicated to saving endangered and valuable iris plants but had not mentioned the monetary value of her iris plants.

According to Anita, Joan was a master gardener who grew irises and herbs. She was the one who introduced Anita to the medicinal benefits of herbs.

Alex grew tomatoes, basil and other herbs. He used them to make the best spaghetti sauce I ever tasted.

Did underlying health conditions play any part in the death of my friends?

At lunch last year, Anita had said Joan became dizzy in the garden but made no mention of any health problems. You may remember that when I asked my friends about Joan's bocce skill they gave conflicting information. They probably would also have a hard time remembering her health.

I know Alex had diabetes; his illness or his medication might have made him dizzy and caused him to stumble and fall. On the other hand, he seemed to be in really good shape; his balance appeared to be excellent in class and on the bocce court the day before he died. Was he exploring other health remedies like herbal elixirs which might have made him dizzy?

Anita had severe headaches and high blood pressure and had recently started a new medication. She was also using herbal supplements from her garden.

Could Anita accidentally have poisoned herself with her herbs? Could her death be a reaction to her new medication? Was it part of whatever was causing her headaches?

Or could my friends have been murdered?

Chapter 29

I needed to clear my head and take a break from trying to figure out if my friends at Golden Oaks had been murdered.

Painting is my favorite way of relaxing. All worries and thoughts of things that should be done just disappear. Kika and I made plans to paint at a beautiful arboretum not far from here.

I decided to have poached eggs for breakfast. After I prepared tea and toast, I looked at the counter and realized I had forgotten to cook the eggs – they were still in the carton. Was this something to worry about? I may have mentioned that I do have some concern about memory problems.

I decided to cook the eggs anyway. I cracked two organic free-range eggs into my Quiko egg cooker. It only takes about 7 minutes to make great poached or soft-boiled eggs. Hard-boiled eggs take a little longer but the shells just slide off. You really should try a Quiko egg cooker sometime.

I didn't care if the tea got cold; bathrooms were still not open due to coronavirus restrictions, so the less tea the better.

We arrived at the arboretum about 9:30. It was a cool, cloudy day and the flowers were lovely. I did a small oil painting showing a gardener at work surrounded by tall blue flowers with an ivy covered building in the distance. After the paint dries I will probably sell the painting and you may be able to purchase it if you do a search on Etsy.

After we finished painting, Kika and I walked around to take photos. Most of the plants were labelled, and I noticed that some of them were poisonous.

Several horticulturists were busy weeding and planting. I approached one of them and asked, "Can you tell me about the poisonous plants growing in that bed?"

She said, "Oh yes, they are very interesting! Some poisonous plants are beautiful but you have to be very careful when you work with them. In some cases, the flowers are edible but the stems and leaves are poisonous to eat. Other plants can kill you if you simply touch them." She continued, "Of course we don't have any of the extremely dangerous plants here."

I asked, "If you wanted to kill someone would you make an elixir from a poisonous plant or would it be better to bake it in a pie?" She looked at me a little strangely and moved away to work in another section of the garden without answering my question. Perhaps I should have been less direct.

When I got home that afternoon I checked "poisonous plants" on google. I had never heard of most of the ones google found and I spent several fascinating hours reading about them. I had forgotten that Socrates was killed by poison hemlock.

My favorite was Cerbera Odollam (also called the suicide tree). A few seeds can poison a dish and the poison is not detectable by toxicology tests. Of course it doesn't grow in New York and I'm not sure how anyone would get the seeds.

Monkshood is lovely and can kill in as little as four hours if you simply touch it. Other possibilities include oleander, morning glory and nightshade. Even rhubarb can be fatal if you eat the leaves – there is a lot of rhubarb in the community garden. The picture of Foxglove, with its tall clusters of small delicately colored blossoms, looked like plants I have seen in the Golden Oaks community gardens.

As I read the list of poisonous plants, an ad for an app called **WhatPlant?** popped up on my phone. This app can identify plants, flowers and weeds. I installed it on my phone immediately.

CHAPTER 30

I haven't had much experience with apps and need to learn how to use **WhatPlant?** in order to find out about the herbs Anita and Ella were growing.

Speaking of apps, some artist friends have art apps on their tablets, and I'm impressed with the interesting work they create. One of the members of my Tuesday art group, Renee, is a very serious artist who usually works in her studio, using her iPad. She says she sometimes loses track of time for hours working on her designs.

Occasionally I can talk her into painting with me outdoors, and one day she agreed to go to the community garden to paint the summer flowers that were in full bloom. My real motive was to check out the garden for clues, but I didn't mention this to Renee. There's no point in frightening people with talk of murder or calling attention to my investigation.

Renee did very lovely detailed botanical drawings of several flowers, including a black iris, and took photos to use if she decided to do a painting later.

I found some very interesting flowers in Ella's garden that I had never seen before and sketched them in some detail. I always carry a sketch pad and have drawings of almost everything that goes on around Golden Oaks. I often review my sketches for ideas for paintings and sometimes just to remember what's been happening. Before we left, I painted a quick watercolor of an iris in Ella's garden. My painting looks a little like a flower if you squint from across the room.

In our next art group Renee carefully looked at the paintings she had done in the garden and identified the various flowers. My first reaction was, "Who cares about that? Paintings should not look exactly like the flower! Their name is totally unimportant!" Of course I did not say this out loud because I am making an effort to be more tactful.

When I got home I pulled out the painting I had done of the iris in Ella's garden. I tried using **WhatPlant?** but got no information – it only works with photos not paintings.

The next day I went back to Anita's garden and took photos to use with **WhatPlant?**. I decided to start with the irises. Did you know that the iris was named after the Greek goddess who rode rainbows?

WhatPlant? identified several irises in Anita's garden. She had seven Purple Tall Bearded Irises, four Stairway to Heaven Irises and three Immortality Irises. But I couldn't find the Hester Prynne Iris that Anita had been so proud of at our last lunch. It should have been easy to spot with its dark purple and lavender colors with yellow accents.

I then used **WhatPlant?** to identify Anita's herbs. She had the usual basil, parsley, dill and chives. There were no poisonous herbs but she did have rhubarb which has poisonous leaves and there was a Foxglove plant tucked among the herbs.

Chapter 31

I remembered that Anita had mentioned that Ella was a master gardener who shared her interest in herbs. They had been giving each other various herbs and exchanging recipes for using them

I almost never see Ella around campus. She is a short, chunky woman with very pale skin and jet black hair. She usually works in her garden at dusk and may be trying to avoid bright sun because of her fair skin. I think she also tries to avoid people because she usually scurries away when I arrive in the garden. In one of our few conversations last year, I offered her some kale and she accepted. Most people just cringe when I offer them kale.

That evening I went to the garden in hopes

of seeing Ella and was delighted that she was there. She was kneeling on the ground doing some weeding. I decided to start by asking her advice about herbs.

"Hi Ella, isn't this a nice time of day to work in the garden? At least it's not so hot," I babbled on a little nervously. She looked up in surprise but continued pulling weeds without answering. I went on: "Your flowers are lovely and the colors harmonize so well." She stopped weeding and gazed lovingly around her garden.

"Do you think it's too late in the season to put in some herbs? I have that garden in the corner and need a few more plants." I pointed in the general direction of my garden and she turned to look. She seemed somewhat interested and replied, "No, some kinds of herbs can be planted almost anytime. What would you like to use them for?"

I explained, "I want herbs that taste good in sauces. And I've been feeling a little tired lately. I've heard that some of them improve energy. Do you have any recommendations?"

Ella was almost enthusiastic in talking about the benefits of herbs. She recommended basil and rosemary for tomato sauces and dill for white sauces. Her excitement rose as she talked about the positive effect some herbs can have on health. She patted a few plants fondly as she spoke.

I glanced around her garden as we talked and complimented her on several lovely flowers. Then I noticed an unusual plant. "I've never seen a plant quite like that one. What kind is it? It's very pretty." She seemed to become uncomfortable and said she was not sure what kind it was.

Then I noticed another flower. It was dark purple with yellow spots and looked like the iris Anita had been so excited about. I decided not to mention it to Ella. It was almost dark, so I headed for home without watering my garden. I thought I had made a good start with Ella even though I had not mentioned Anita or Joan or asked if she had seen anything suspicious.

I went back to the garden the next morning to take pictures of some of Ella's herbs and the iris that looked a little like Anita's. I jumped at the sound of a voice behind me, "What are you doing? Those are my flowers!" It was Ella, and she looked very annoyed.

I tried to sound casual. "Oh hi, Ella," I said. "I

thought your flowers were so beautiful that I wanted photos of them to use as a reference for my paintings."

She looked unconvinced and moved closer to me. I explained, "I'm an artist and I'm painting a series of the beautiful trees and flowers at Golden Oaks; your flowers would be perfect."

I find that it's easier to tell a lie when I stick somewhat close to the truth and, as you know, I really did try to paint a series during social distancing. Of course, I have almost stopped the series but who's to know that?

As I told my useful lie, I flashed back to Carol's story about writing an article for a nursing magazine. This will need more thought.

I tried to get in Ella's good graces and rambled on a bit about selling paintings on Etsy. Then I asked "How do you manage to grow such lovely irises?" She still did not look happy but told me a little about fertilizer and the way to water.

Anita had mentioned that Ella was in the garden when Joan became ill last year. I wasn't sure if it was important but wanted to explore this idea. So I asked, "Do you remember Joan? She and Anita both loved irises and were trying to save endangered plants." Ella glared at me and turned away and went back to pulling weeds.

I was beginning to think Ella might be a suspect rather than a source of information. But why would she care about any plant enough to kill? Were they that valuable? She did have a few herbs that could be dangerous. But were they lethal? Even if she were to make a poisonous liquid, how could she get anybody to drink it?

CHAPTER 32

I decided that I might find some clues around Ella's apartment. The next evening when I was pretty sure she would be in the garden, I walked up the trail to her apartment. She lives in 308 Mountain Top at the top of the hill next to the woods.

The garden around her home was perfectly manicured. In the front of the house were beautiful azaleas and peonies and some annual flowers. It was very neat and orderly – she must spend a lot of time working on it to make sure that everything is in such good shape.

In the back of her house was a flower bed with lovely irises and several beautiful flowers that I had not seen anywhere else on campus. I also recognized several poisonous plants mixed in with the flowers.

I was standing at a distance, close to the woods, but was able to zoom in and take several photos. I didn't want to spend any more time than necessary at her apartment in case she returned.

When I got back to my own apartment I checked the app **WhatPlant**? and learned that the iris in Ella's garden was one of Anita's most prized flowers. Of course it's very possible that both Ella and Anita had gotten a specimen of this particular iris.

Chapter 33

Wednesday was very hot, but by 8:00 pm it had cooled a little. I went up to the garden and was pleased that Ella was there. As usual, I stopped for a chat and as usual, she was not happy to see me.

I knew that my photos and drawings of her flowers had upset her. I had my sketchbook with me and offered her two sketches, one of her garden and another of one of her irises. She looked at both carefully and seemed pleased.

I told her about my painting trip to the arboretum, and said that I was thinking of writing a book about the lovely flowers throughout the state. I held out my phone to show her a photo I had taken of a beautiful iris there. It was dramatic – purple with bright red stripes and yellow spots. Ella glanced at it and seemed to become nervous.

I decided that there was no point in continuing the conversation and went to my own garden to work. After a few minutes I sat on the ground and put my head down.

Ella must have been watching because she came over right away. "Are you all right?" she asked, sounding very concerned.

"Just a little dizzy," I replied.

She reached in her pocket and pulled out a small bottle. "Here," she said, "Try this. I think it will help you."

"Thank you." I said weakly. I raised the bottle to my nose and detected a very sweet odor. "This smells wonderful. What is it?" I asked.

"It's a special blend of herbs from my garden. I drink some every day and it makes me feel wonderful," she replied.

I pretended to take a sip then leaned back for a secybit. Then I sat up slowly and said, "I am feeling much better already – my head has stopped swimming." I screwed the bottle cap on tight, and said, "Thank you. That drink really did the trick."

She reached for the bottle and said, "Oh in that case let me take it back – I can drink it later myself."

I said, "No, I'll take it home and finish it later. I might even get your recipe and use it every day. Thank you again."

She looked as though she wanted to grab it from my hand but (maybe because I am about a foot taller) decided against it.

CHAPTER 34

I called the kids, and we talked on Jane's phone. I brought them up to date about my conversations with Ella and the drink she gave me. They agreed that she was acting very suspiciously and thought I should get the drink analyzed to see if it contains poison.

Roger said, "Be sure to activate the trap at your house in case she comes down there."

Jeff agreed and added, "Don't forget to keep your doors locked and use the peephole before you let anyone in."

Jane said, "She certainly seems to know you suspect her. But we can't be sure yet what really happened, so it's important to talk to her again."

The boys agreed but Roger added that he

didn't think I should go to her house alone. "Can you ask a friend to go with you?" Jeff asked.

Before talking to Ella, I wanted to get more information. Mr. Andrews had been no help. He did not seem to think that there was a problem or at least did not want to discuss it with me.

So I decided to see Mrs. Michaels, the director of admissions. She has worked at Golden Oaks for many years and in fact I knew her when my father lived here. She has always been extremely helpful to all the residents.

I dropped into her office – no need for an appointment. I told her about the deaths of Anita, Alex and Joan and explained my concern that they may have been murdered. I mentioned my feeling that Mr. Andrews had not been willing to consider the possibility that there may have been foul play.

Mrs. Michaels was well aware of the deaths but had not considered the possibility that something out of the ordinary had happened. Her first comment was that Mr. Andrews was correct that some residents do die unexpectedly and others die after a fall. But on the other hand, she seemed quite concerned

Murder? A Memoir

about having a possible murderer on the loose at Golden Oaks. She appeared worried about the safety of the residents and also the reputation of the facility. Murder would not encourage anyone to move here.

I told Mrs. Michaels that I had talked to Ella in the garden several times and that she had offered me a drink when I said I felt dizzy. I said I still had the drink and wanted to have it analyzed.

Mrs. Michaels shared some information with me and told me that Ella's husband had died suddenly shortly before she moved here. Her two children live fairly close and are concerned about her and visit often. The information about Ella's husband is another angle that I will need to consider carefully.

I said it was possible that there was a good explanation and that Ella was completely innocent. In order to clear the matter up I would need to have a serious talk with Ella.

I told Mrs. Michaels that I was a little nervous because Ella's reactions yesterday seemed agitated and perhaps aggressive. Mrs. Michaels agreed that another conversation would be a good idea and offered to go with me. I accepted her offer right away. Mrs.

148

Michaels is very calm; her presence might reassure Ella.   She would also be a good witness if we need to involve the police.

Chapter 35

I decided to telephone Ella to set up an appointment. After a few rings, her answering machine picked up. Her message was simple: "I'm not here, Leave a message at the beep."

I took a deep breath and left a message. "Hi Ella, this is Cate May. We were talking in the garden yesterday. It's urgent that I talk to you about a few things. I'll stop by at 3:00 tomorrow and bring Mrs. Michaels with me to help us figure out what is going on."

Mrs. Michaels and I arrived at Ella's apartment promptly at 3:00. She did not answer the door. I pulled out my cell phone and called her. My call went directly to her answering machine.

"Hi Ella," I said. "It's Cate. I'm sorry we missed you. Please give me a call when you have time and we can set up another visit."

When I got home there was a message on my machine from Ella. "I'm sorry I wasn't able to keep our appointment. I am very sorry for everything and hope you will understand."

The next day I learned that Ella had died suddenly during the night. Everyone was upset at her death, and nobody seemed to know if she had heart problems or any other health issues that might explain her sudden death.

Lynn said, "That's at least the fourth person who died suddenly and no one knows what was wrong with them."

Phyllis replied, "Yes, it's like a streak – first was Joan, then Anita, and Alex and now Ella. When will it end? We survived Covid, but now people are dropping dead. It makes you wonder what is going on and how many more of us are going to die."

But I knew that we had reached the end of the streak of death.

CHAPTER 36

That afternoon I decided to return to Ella's apartment. I walked around the outside and everything appeared in order although there were some freshly planted irises. Then I noticed that the poisonous plants in the back were gone. In their place were brightly colored geraniums.

I reviewed all my sketches and notes, cutting things out and physically moving them around to see where they fit best. This is what I do when I make an abstract painting and use collage. Just moving something to another location can give everything a whole new meaning.

I know Ella gave Joan a drink just before she had been taken by ambulance to the hospital where she died. I also know that Ella and Anita had been sharing herbal elixirs and that Anita was desperately seeking relief from her headaches. It is certainly possible that Ella had offered Anita a drink that she said would lessen her headaches.

The problem remains that I haven't found a motive for her to kill anyone. The iris plants were said to be rare and valuable. But I don't know how she would go about selling them. There were several irises by her back door that may have been taken from Anita's garden. Could it be that she just wanted to have rare and beautiful specimens in her garden?

It's possible that she gave Alex a poisonous drink, but did she have any motive to kill him? His garden was next to hers, but he grew only tomatoes and kitchen herbs. The only possible explanation I could see was that he somehow became suspicious and asked her too many questions. Or perhaps his death really was a coincidence and he died after a simple fall.

Chapter 37

The only way to prove that foul play had been involved would be to open police investigations on all three possible victims and have autopsies performed. That would detect most poisons but not Cerbera Odollam although of course those seeds would have been very difficult to obtain.

I had attended both Anita and Alex's funerals and spoken to their families. They seem to have come to terms with the death of their parents. Would they be happier knowing their parents had been murdered?

Joan died almost two years ago. I had never met her family, but it's hard to imagine they would want an investigation now.

Ella's funeral was private so I had no

opportunity to talk to her two children. How would they feel when an investigation proved that their mother was a murderer? According to Ella's obituary, she was a former hospice nurse who was dedicated to helping people in their last few weeks of life. Did this play any role?

An investigation would not be easy. You may remember that some residents get a little confused and have a hard time giving detailed descriptions. I didn't learn much when I questioned my friends about Joan, and they would get even more flustered if a detective was asking the questions.

How would a police investigation affect Golden Oaks? I realized I love it here in spite of Ted and a few other difficult people. Social distancing in my former home with no close neighbors would have been dull indeed.

There are more empty apartments than usual, and I believe that Golden Oaks would like to get back to full occupancy. It surely would not be good publicity to have the murder of several residents in the news.

All in all, what would be solved by a police investigation? In the end I decided to do nothing. I emptied the bottle of elixir Ella had given me on the ground near my patio; I didn't want to risk pouring poison down the drain where it might get into the water supply. The next day I noticed that the grass by my patio had started to turn brown.

A few days later when I was chatting with friends in the lobby, Mrs. Michaels walked by and said, "Cate, do you have a minute to talk?" I followed her to her office and took a seat.

Mrs. Michaels shuffled through a small pile of papers on her desk and said, "I want to bring you up to date about Ella. When we inspected her apartment we found several lists – a shopping list, a list of flowers and a list of people."

After a pause, Mrs. Michaels continued, "I thought you should know that your name was on her list of people."

"Oh," I said, "Were Joan, Anita and Alex on that list too? How many other residents were on it?"

"I'm sorry, Cate. I can't give you any more information. But I thought you should know about the lists." Then she added, "We also found a drawing of her garden that was signed by you. It looked like Ella was in the process of framing it."

Mrs. Michaels smiled warmly and said, "Thank you for your help."

Always quick to pick up on subtle cues, I sensed that the conversation and my investigation were over. I thanked Mrs. Michaels and rejoined my friends in the lobby.

Some people at Golden Oaks are a little quirky, but most mean well. And if just this one time quirkiness crossed into murder I might be able to accept it. Maybe when you reach a certain age you realize that a little bit of uncertainty may be for the best. In my paintings I try to capture a mood, but details can get in the way of seeing the big picture. Maybe life is somewhat like an impressionistic painting.

How can I explain to Jane, Jeff and Roger that I am not going to pursue the investigation? I will attach these notes to my will. Many years from now when the will is read they will begin to understand. Of course by that time they may have children of their own. They will certainly have benefited from my wisdom and the critical thinking skills they have developed through our investigation.

ACKNOWLEDGMENTS

I've always thought a murder mystery should end with a confession, so here is mine. This book is a combination of fact and fiction. The murders are purely a product of my imagination. The year 2020 with the Covid-19 pandemic, social distancing and political unrest actually occurred.

Most characters are a blend of people I have met through the years and bear little semblance to reality. Several of my friends volunteered to be in the story and chose their names. I hope they will still be my friends if they read this book. My intent was to create an impression of the friendly, quirky people in a retirement community such as Golden Oaks. I had no interest in being accurate or giving realistic descriptions of anyone. As I often say when painting, accuracy and perfection are highly overrated.

Although my son and daughter-in-law are minor characters in the book they play a major role in my life and their help and support are greatly appreciated.

I want to thank my grandchildren who are even more wonderful than described and are responsible for this book. When I visited during 2020 I said I wanted to write a mystery but needed a plot. They wanted to hear about my friends and discussed who should be the killer. Every day before they went to the basement for virtual school, they told me to write a chapter. By the time I returned home the book had taken on life and they became co-detectives. My 11 year old granddaughter designed the book cover and coached me in writing conversation.

I'd also like to thank those who read drafts of the book and offered suggestions and encouragement when I almost gave up, particularly my sister and brother. Also thanks to my proofreader friend for suggestions about punctuation and continuity.

ABOUT THE AUTHOR

This is the first novella by Susan Sumner. Her second book, Murder, Art and Gelato, will be released later this year.

Susan is a prolific painter and former social worker. She is co-author of a software program that helps teachers prepare lesson plans for special education students.

Like Cate May, she is 85 years old and lives in a retirement complex where she is an acute and loving observer of life. In both writing and painting she aims for impressions rather than accurate portraits.

You may contact the author at susanksumner@gmail.com if you want any information or are interested in developing a film based on the book. Helen Mirren or Jane Fonda would be good possibilities for the part of Cate May.

Made in United States
North Haven, CT
20 October 2021